Most people don't thin~~k~~ ~~they~~ ~~don't~~
think why. They shout things like, "Spud, get
out of there!" – just because I've turned their
dustbins over or dug their flowerbeds up.
Can't they see it's fun? Geraldine says
humans have a different sense of humour
to dogs, but you'd think they'd learn . . .

YOUNG CORGI BOOKS

Young Corgi books are perfect when you are looking for great books to read on your own. They are full of exciting stories and entertaining pictures. There are funny books, scary books, spine-tingling stories and mysterious ones. Whatever your interests you'll find something in Young Corgi to suit you: from families to football, from animals to ghosts. The books are written by some of the most famous and popular of today's children's authors, and by some of the best new talents, too.

Whether you read one chapter a night, or devour the whole book in one sitting, you'll love Young Corgi books. The more you read, the more you'll want to read!

Other Young Corgi books to get your teeth into
Boojer by Alison Prince,
Bumble by Alison Prince
Titus Rules OK by Dick King-Smith
The Railway Angel by Joyce Dunbar
Robomum by Emily Smith

To Lettice Philomena,
who saw it first

SPUD
A YOUNG CORGI BOOK: 0 552 549088

Published in Great Britain by Young Corgi Books
an imprint of Random House Children's Books

This edition published 2003

1 3 5 7 9 10 8 6 4 2

Papers used by Random House Children's Books are natural,
recyclable products made from wood grown in sustainable forests.
The manufacturing processes conform to the environmental regulations
of the country of origin.

Set in 17/21pt Bembo Schoolbook by
Falcon Oast Graphic Art Ltd.

Young Corgi Books are published by Random House Children's Books,
61–63 Uxbridge Road, London W5 5SA,
a division of The Random House Group Ltd,
in Australia by Random House Australia (Pty) Ltd,
20 Alfred Street, Milsons Point, Sydney, NSW 2061, Australia,
in New Zealand by Random House New Zealand Ltd,
18 Poland Road, Glenfield, Auckland 10, New Zealand
and in South Africa by Random House (Pty) Ltd,
Endulini, 5a Jubilee Road, Parktown 2192, South Africa

THE RANDOM HOUSE GROUP Limited Reg. No. 954009
www.**kids**at**randomhouse**.co.uk

A CIP catalogue record for this book is available from the British Library

Printed and bound in Great Britain by
Cox & Wyman Ltd, Reading, Berkshire

SPUD

ALISON PRINCE

Illustrated by Kate Sheppard

YOUNG CORGI

Chapter One
Turkey

Mrs Piffey is great. She doesn't mind me jumping on the chairs or bringing in old bones, and she leaves the back door open all day so I can go in and out. That way, I do what I like and she can get on with her hairdressing.

Lots of ladies come to her front room to get their hair done. They have it washed and cut and pinned up in rollers, and then they sit under hot-air blowers, reading magazines. Men come too sometimes. The boy who drives the fish van has orange-coloured hair, slicked down with gel, and I think he looks like a kipper.

Mrs Piffey calls her front room "the salon". I'm not allowed in there any more, not since I was sick on the floor after I'd eaten some curry I found in a bin. The ladies got upset, and Mrs Piffey said I was banned.

I didn't mind much — there was nothing to eat in the salon, anyway. I tried a plastic roller once, but it gave me hiccups, and those stinky shampoos and hairsprays made me sneeze. And there are lots of nicer things to do.

I like teasing Blanco, for instance. He's white and fluffy, and his owners keep him in behind a fence all the time, so he goes berserk when he's barked at. But Geraldine is even better, because she's so nervous. She's taller than me, with black wool all over, but if I bounce out at her from under the hedge, she shrieks and falls down. It's the same every time — her legs just fold up, and it always makes me laugh. Geraldine belongs to a girl called Rosie who thinks I'm sweet. She gives me a dog chew sometimes.

9

Most people don't think I'm sweet – I can't think why. They shout things like, "Spud, get out of there!" – just because I've turned their dustbins over or dug their flowerbeds up. Can't they see it's fun? Geraldine says humans have a different sense of humour to dogs, but you'd think they'd learn.

I was born in a greengrocer's shop.
There weren't any bins or flowerbeds
in there, just lots of vegetables. There
were five of us puppies, and the
greengrocer called us:

Bean, Sprout,

Cauli, Cu

and Spud.

That's my name, Spud. When my
sister Cauli went to her new home her
owners called her Sheba, because they
said we weren't Collie dogs. We knew
that, of course. We're Blooming
Scroungers. At least, that's what the
greengrocer said.

Mrs Piffey didn't change my name.

We got on well right from the start. We'd sit side by side on the sofa in the evenings, watching telly, me with a bone and Mrs Piffey with her chocolates. She says chocolate is bad for dogs, but that's OK with me. I like bones better anyway, specially ones I've buried. They have a nice, ripe flavour.

One evening, while we were sitting there, the phone rang. I didn't take any notice — it rings all the time, with people wanting to come and have their hair done. But Mrs Piffey got all excited.

"*Turkey?*" she said.

"Darling, do you really mean it?"

I pricked up my ears. I knew all about turkey. We'd had it for Christmas, and it's very tasty. I started to dribble a bit, just thinking about it.

"For two whole weeks?" Mrs Piffey was saying. "How wonderful!"

I thought it must be a very big

turkey, to last us for two weeks. I dribbled even more. But then Mrs Piffey gave me a worried glance and said, "What about Spud?"

I wagged my tail, but she wasn't looking. "Darling, he'd *hate* kennels," she said. "He's used to going in and out as he likes."

Darling said something else and Mrs Piffey nodded seriously. "Turkey or Spud," she said. "It's my choice. Yes, I do see."

Turkey *or* Spud? Whatever could she mean? Why not both? I pushed my nose in her ear, but she just patted me and wiped the dribble off absent-mindedly. "I'm sure someone will have him," she said. Then she started talking about things called kebabs and belly-dancing, and I couldn't work out what was going on.

Chapter Two
Geraldine

The next morning Mrs Piffey kept looking at me in a worried kind of way. Then the first hairdressing lady arrived, and she went off into the salon.

I felt worried, too. I went down the road and barked at Blanco, and he jumped up and down, yapping like a maniac, but it didn't seem as much fun as usual. I was still thinking about Mrs Piffey and the turkey. I went back home and listened outside the door of the salon.

"Spud's quite a friendly dog, really," one of the ladies was saying. "I'd take him, only I don't think I could manage him."

"You don't have to manage him," Mrs Piffey said. "He manages himself."

"That's just it," said another lady. "I'd worry all the time about what he was up to. And anyway," she added, "I'm going to the Scillies with my sister."

I wondered what kind of sillies she meant. Were they going to walk on their hands, with hats on their feet? Or sit in trees like silly cats that have run up and can't get down?

"They grow daffodils, don't they?" Mrs Piffey said, but I didn't understand that, either. Why were daffodils silly?

Then the ladies went on talking about me. "There's always Mrs Cats-Home," one of them said. "She takes dogs as well as cats. She's mad about animals."

"Just plain mad, if you ask me," another lady said. "Those weird clothes."

"I don't mind how mad she is," said Mrs Piffey, "but Spud chases cats, and I don't think she'd have him." She sighed. "Turkey was a nice idea, but it's probably a dead duck."

I knew about duck. It was even nicer than turkey. Sitting outside the door, I started to dribble again.

"Give him to Mavis Crumm," said the lady who was going to be silly. "She'll lick him into shape. She knows all about dogs."

Mrs Piffey sighed again. "She doesn't know about Spud," she said.

There was a pause, then the first lady said, "I'll have him." She sounded very brave.

"Oh, Elsie, would you?" said Mrs Piffey. "That's really sweet of you."

I felt more worried than ever. I didn't see why someone called Elsie was going to have me, or why I couldn't share the turkey with Mrs Piffey. Or the duck. Something had gone badly wrong. I didn't want to hear any more, so I went out through the back door and wandered down the road.

Without really meaning to, I found myself at Rosie's house. Rosie was bending over a pen in the garden, feeding dandelion leaves to a lot of rabbits, and Geraldine was watching from behind a watering can. She's scared of rabbits – she says they might bite her ankles. I sneaked up and gave her a nudge, and she shrieked and fell down as usual. I grinned.

"Oh, Spud, you are naughty," said Rosie, but she wasn't really cross – she never is. "Geraldine, stand up, you're all right – don't be ridiculous."

Geraldine got to
her feet and gave
me a sheepish
smile. She always
looks sheepish,
because of having
wool all over, but she's
quite nice, really.

Rosie finished with the dandelion
leaves and dusted her hands. "Now
we'll go for a walk," she said. "Do you
want to come, Spud?"

I prefer being on my own really,
because I like looking in people's bins
or getting into their kitchens if I'm
lucky, but this time I went along with
Rosie and Geraldine. I needed
someone to talk to.

"Oh, you poor thing," Geraldine
said when I told her about Mrs Piffey
and the turkey. "You're going to be
given away. That's what happened to

me. The people I used to live with went to a place they called Oz, and they said I couldn't come. They gave me to Mrs Cats-Home. I stayed there for ages, until Rosie's family came and got me."

That was rubbish, of course – Mrs Piffey would never give me away. But then, Geraldine isn't the brightest of dogs. "No, she's going to have this turkey," I told her. "With Darling."

Geraldine thought hard, then said, "They might be going somewhere else for the turkey."

This was true, of course, but it didn't help. "I think it's Darling's turkey," I said. "And he doesn't like me much, because I ate his slippers. But I could stay on the sofa with a bone and the telly. Why do I have to go to Elsie? For two whole weeks?"

"Well," said Geraldine, "they could be taking the turkey to Oz." And then she trod on a prickle and went totally hysterical, and Rosie had to come and sort her out. Like I say, Geraldine really doesn't have much brain.

Chapter Three
Elsie

Mrs Piffey started to behave very oddly. She tried on funny-looking glasses with dark brown glass in them, and bought a lot of skimpy tops and bottoms that didn't cover much of her, and she kept looking at herself in the mirror and saying she'd have to go on a diet. She bought a new camera, too, and took some photos of me to make sure she knew how it worked, and I heard her talking to the ladies in the salon about sun block, whatever that was.

Then one morning, just after I'd had my breakfast, she washed my bowl and put it in her shopping basket together with a bag of dog meal and a lot of tins. We hadn't used my lead for years, but she hunted about in drawers and cupboards until she found it, and clipped it to my collar.

"We're going to see Elsie," she said.

If I hadn't been on the lead I'd have gone somewhere else until she forgot the idea, but there was no choice. Off we went to Elsie's house, which was dreadfully clean and tidy. "Now, Spud, you're to be a good boy," Mrs Piffey said.

"He'll be fine," said Elsie. "Just you enjoy Turkey and don't worry about a thing."

I tried to sneak out with Mrs Piffey when she left, but Elsie held onto my collar and shut the door. I could hear Mrs Piffey going down the garden path without me.

"It's only for a fortnight," Elsie told me. "It'll soon go." She sounded hopeful, but I just wanted Mrs Piffey to come back. I lay down with my nose to the crack under the door and waited.

Lunch time came and went, and I still lay there. Elsie tried to give me a biscuit, but I didn't eat it.

"Perhaps you want to Do Something," she said. So she let me out.

I burrowed under her fence and went straight back to Mrs Piffey's, but it was all different. The kitchen door was shut, and I couldn't get in. The flowered curtains were drawn across the window of the salon and there was no hum of hot-air machines and no radio playing.

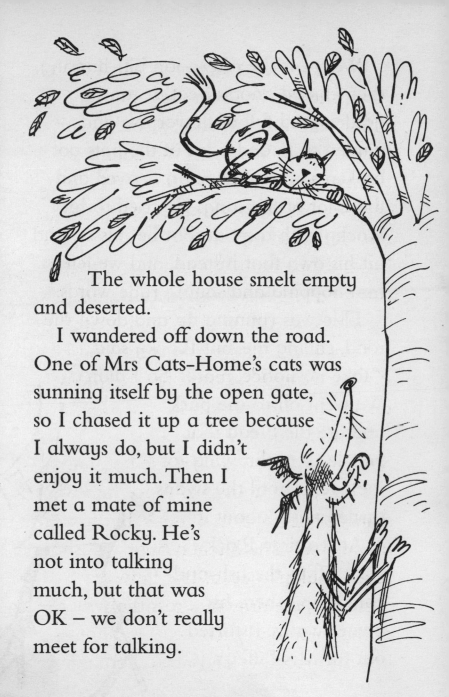

The whole house smelt empty and deserted.

I wandered off down the road. One of Mrs Cats-Home's cats was sunning itself by the open gate, so I chased it up a tree because I always do, but I didn't enjoy it much. Then I met a mate of mine called Rocky. He's not into talking much, but that was OK – we don't really meet for talking.

We spent the afternoon bin-hunting, then chased another cat. It ran into a garden shed full of flowerpots and garden stuff, and a lot of the pots got broken somehow. A man arrived and did a lot of shouting. He tried to hit Rocky with a spade, but he missed and hit his own foot instead, and we left him hopping and saying rude words.

Elsie was running up and down the road, calling me, but Rocky said, "Take no notice, mate." So I didn't. We went off to the park and ate the bread that people were throwing for the swans, until the swans turned nasty about it.

At tea time Rocky went off to the fish-and-chip shop, where his owner works. I started out for Mrs Piffey's house, but I met a little kid who was bawling at his mum because he didn't like his ice cream.

I don't want a *pink* one!" he yelled. "I want a *chocolate* one, with *stripes*!" He was trying to kick his mum, and as they passed he tried to kick me as well. His pink ice cream fell out of its cornet, so I ate it. He got even crosser and threw the cornet at me, so I ate that as well, and his mum lugged him off, bellowing.

I was just finishing the cornet when someone grabbed my collar and said, "GOT YOU!"

It was a woman wearing a brown jacket and a headscarf, and Elsie was with her.

"Oh, Mavis, thank you so much," Elsie said to the woman. "I'd never have caught him."

"You just have to be firm," said Mavis. She held my collar all the way back to Elsie's house, then handed me over to Elsie.

Chapter Four
Walks

I was stuck there all night. The next morning Elsie put my lead on, and when I went out, she came too. "Walkies," she said.

I didn't want walkies. I'd planned to look for Mrs Piffey, and taking Elsie along was going to be a nuisance. I charged down the garden path at high speed, but Elsie managed to stop by clinging to the gatepost.

"Wait!" she said. But as soon as she let go of the gatepost I hauled her all the way to Mrs Piffey's house.

It was still closed up and empty. "You see?" said Elsie. "Now, we'll have walkies. In the woods."

I simply couldn't get rid of her. She grabbed at fences and trees to try and slow me down, and she screamed every time I pulled her through a muddy bit, and kept shouting, "Spud, do stop!" When I took her off the path, she got mixed up with some brambles and shrieked about that as well, but she still wouldn't let go. When we got back, she shut me in the kitchen, and I heard her complaining about me to Mavis on the phone.

It was the same the next day. She kept hanging onto my lead, even though she fell in the stream when I went for a swim. She was only in as far as her knees, but she made such a fuss, you'd have thought she was drowning. I felt a

bit sorry for her after that, so I showed
her how to shake herself dry, but she
stood too close and got showered.

She met one of the hairdressing
ladies while I was taking her home.

The lady looked at us and said,
"Oh, dear. Is he giving you a difficult
time?"

Elsie wiped some mud off her face
and said, "Honestly, Fiona, if I'd
realized what he's like, I'd never have
offered."

"Oh, what a shame," said Fiona. "Tell you what – I've got one of those very long leads, from when I had Midge. It's the telescopic sort, in a plastic handle. I'll bring it round, if you like."

"That would be wonderful," said Elsie.

I saw a squirrel and went after it, and Elsie lost her balance because she was still attached to me by the lead. She clutched Fiona, and both of them fell over. I couldn't pull the pair of them very far, so the squirrel got away. It ran up a tree and said a lot of rude squirrel-words, which was very annoying.

The next day Elsie put me on the long lead. I quite liked it because I could get further away from her, but she didn't like it a bit. Every time I went through a blackberry bush or under some twiggy stuff or round a tree, the string got mixed up in the stalks and branches, and she had to come and sort it out.

Then she got completely stuck in a boggy bit and couldn't move. I jumped over a big rock, and the lead broke. *Brilliant*, I thought. I was free at last.

I spent the rest of the day looking for Mrs Piffey. I looked in the queue at the bus stop and in the shops and went to all the houses I could think of where she might be. I even called at Mrs Cats-Home, where all the cats spat and hissed, but there was no sign of her. I'd have looked in Darling's house, too, only I didn't know where he lived. He always arrived in a car.

Rocky joined me after that. We found a dead pigeon and I forgot about Mrs Piffey for a bit. There's nothing so delicious as the scent of week-old pigeon, specially when you've rolled on it for a long time and got it well rubbed into your fur. I went to share the aroma with Geraldine, and she almost fainted because it was so wonderful. I had another look at Mrs Piffey's house, but it was still shut up and empty, so I went back to Elsie's because I was getting hungry.

The lovely perfume of pigeon was
wasted on Elsie. In face, she screamed
and buried her nose in a handkerchief,
and her eyes were running. She rang
up Fiona, who came round at once,
and the pair of them ran a bath
that smelled like the stuff in Mrs
Piffey's salon. Then they put
me in it.

By the time they'd finished shampooing and scrubbing, they'd totally ruined the scent of pigeon. My fur stank of shampoo and I stood there shivering while they dried me with a hairdryer.

"Honestly, Elsie, this dog is a bit much," said Fiona.

"I know," said Elsie, tugging at my ears with a comb. "I've had enough. I'm going to give him to Mavis Crumm."

Chapter Five
Mavis

Mavis came round the next morning in a car that was already full of dogs. "STAY!" she shouted at them, then added to me, "In you hop, Sunshine."

So in I hopped. Anything would be better than Elsie and the shampoo.

"Thank you *so* much," Elsie said to Mavis. "I do hope he won't be a nuisance."

"Oh, we'll soon get him licked into shape," said Mavis, and drove off.

Her dogs were a funny lot. There were two Afghan hounds who stared down their noses all the time, an ordinary black one who looked a bit gloomy, three small ones with brown blotches and a spaniel who gazed at

Mavis with constant love and admiration. Sick-making, really.

I asked, "Where are we going?" but they didn't answer. "Come on," I said, "you must know."

"Home," muttered the black one, "but we're not supposed to make a noise, so shut up."

None of the others said a word. I never met such a stuffy lot. We arrived at a house that had a big shed in the garden, and the other dogs went to the door of the shed and waited to be let in. I doubled back to the gate, hoping to get out, but Mavis grabbed me and hauled me into her kitchen.

She put a folded
blanket on the floor beside
the cooker, then pointed
at it and said, "BED."

It wasn't bed time, so I didn't take
any notice. I went and looked in the
bin instead, and Mavis whacked me
across the nose with a folded
newspaper and roared, "NO! BAD DOG!"

This place was no fun at all. I sat
down, feeling gloomy. "That's better,"
Mavis said. She gave me a choc-drop,
and I ate it because Elsie hadn't given
me any breakfast, but I decided to
escape as soon as possible. I absolutely
had to find Mrs Piffey.

My chance came when we went for a
walk. It didn't look good at first,
because I was on a lead and Mavis's
dogs weren't. They trotted along beside
her as if they'd never dream of doing

anything else. When we got to the
woods, Mavis said, "Off!" and her dogs
ran about and enjoyed themselves. I
tried to run about as well, but she
wouldn't let me. "Not you, Sunshine,"
she said. "You're not reliable."

I sat down. I wasn't going anywhere
with Mavis. She tugged at my lead
and said, "Come along." But I didn't
come along. I pulled backwards,
shaking my head from side to side.
And I felt my collar start to slip
over one ear.

"Don't you dare!"
shouted Mavis. But
I pulled even
harder, and the
collar came right
off. I ran, needless
to say, and kept
running until I couldn't
hear Mavis shouting any more.

I came out of the woods into some fields, and had an idea. Perhaps Mrs Piffey and Darling had gone for a picnic. We did that once last summer, only Darling was cross because I ate most of the picnic before we got there. How was I to know they wanted to eat ham sandwiches in a field?

Anyway, I had a good look for Mrs Piffey in these fields. She wasn't there, but I found an interesting tent. There was half a loaf inside it, and four sausages and some butter and cheese and a whole packet of biscuits, so when I'd eaten all that I felt nicely full. I lay down in the sun for a little rest and went to sleep. I didn't wake up until the tent people came back and started shouting.

It was almost dark by the time I got back to Mrs Piffey's house, and she still wasn't there. I lay down on our doorstep with my head on my paws.

After a long time someone came along with a torch, but it wasn't Mrs Piffey. It was Mavis.

"There you are," she said. I thought she was going to hit me with a newspaper, but she just buckled on my collar, tighter this time, and took me back to her house.
She opened a tin, and when I'd finished eating, she pointed at the folded blanket and said, "Bed."

There was nothing else to do, so I went and lay on it.

"Good dog," she said. Then she put the light out and left me in the kitchen.

*

When I woke up the next morning, I scratched at the door, but it was firmly shut. There was no hope of going to look for Mrs Piffey. For something else to do, I turned the bin over but there was nothing in it except bits of paper and plastic and empty tins. I started sniffing round the cupboards.

One of them smelt quite interesting, and when I scraped at the door it slid along a bit. I got my nose in and pushed, then my whole head went through.

Elsie's cupboards had been very dull, with nothing in them except saucepans and washing powder, but these were great. There were all sorts of nice packets inside, and I started getting them out to open them on the floor. Some just held

boring things like rice and dry beans
and pasta shapes, but the porridge oats
and sugar were better. I licked some
up from among the other stuff, then
ripped open a packet of raisins, and
they were even nicer. There was a
tub of sticky red cherries, too, so I
ate all those. I bit into a tube of
tomato purée and it came squidging
out like a fat, red worm and got all
over my paws when I trod on it.
Then I got the top off a tin that
had yellow powder inside,
smelling like custard. Neither of
those were much good, but after that
I found some beef stock cubes, and
they were delicious. I was just
starting on a second packet of
them when Mavis came in.

For a moment she stood perfectly still, and her eyes bulged. Then she roared, "YOU BAD DOG!" and reached for a newspaper.

I suddenly felt very nervous, or maybe it was the stock cubes and sticky cherries I'd eaten, but anyway, I started throwing up, all among the other stuff on the floor.

"OUT!" screamed Mavis. She snatched the back door open, and I fled.

Chapter Six
Mrs Cats-Home

When I'd finished being sick, I squeezed
under Mavis's gate, and wandered up
the road to Rosie's house. I was still
feeling rather ill, and I thought
Geraldine would be sympathetic. I
found her in the garden with Rosie
and their cat, Augustus. It's no use
chasing Augustus – he's so fat and lazy
that he never runs away, but I didn't
mind this morning. I wasn't up to
chasing cats.

"Hello, Spud," Rosie said. "Are you
lonely, poor darling? Mrs Piffey's away,
isn't she? Would you like a dog chew?"

I didn't want a dog chew. I couldn't
have eaten anything. I lay down and
groaned, and Rosie looked at me in

concern. "I don't think you're well,"
she said. And she rushed to fetch
her mum.

They both stared at me.

"He's probably eaten something,"
said Rosie's mum. "You know what
he's like. Mrs Piffey feeds him lots, but
he's always looking for more."

"But Mrs Piffey's away and he's
miserable," Rosie wailed. "You can see
he is. Mum, can't he stay here?"

"No, he can't," her mother said.
"We've already got a hamster and a
dog and a cat and twenty-seven
rabbits, and that's enough. And
anyway, Elsie's looking after him. I'll
go and phone her."

Rosie stroked me gently, and I went
on groaning. Then her mum came
back and said, "Elsie couldn't cope
with him. She handed him on to
Mavis Crumm."

"Oh, poor thing," said Rosie.

"So I spoke to Mavis as well," her mother went on, "and she says Spud is the worst dog she's ever known. He's wrecked her kitchen, and she's not having him back."

"So can't we—?"

"Definitely not," said Rosie's mum. "We'll take him round to Mrs Cats-Home."

And they did.

Mrs Cats-Home was wearing something with big flowers all over it, and she had a feather in her hair. Not at all like Mavis.

"Hello, Spud," she said. "Are you coming to stay?"

I gave a sigh and lay down. At least I could chase her cats, once I was feeling better. Maybe even eat their food. I managed to wag my tail.

"Isn't he sweet?" said Rosie.

"Well, I hope so," said Mrs Cats-Home. "I won't have much time to attend to him. I've three more guests arriving this afternoon – two Persians and a goat. And Angela's having kittens."

Rosie clapped her hands. "Kittens! Oh, Mum, couldn't we—?"

"No, we couldn't," said Rosie's mum. And off they went.

There was no way out of Mrs Cats-Home's garden. It had a high wall and the gate was firmly shut across a concrete driveway that I couldn't dig a hole in. The visiting cats lived in a big cage with a cat house and a tree inside, but the ones that belonged to Mrs Cats-Home could go wherever they liked.

By the afternoon I was feeling much better. I ate all the cat food I could find, then chased the cats about, and even the ones in the cage spat and hissed and fluffed themselves up. Two new ones had come, with flat noses and long fur, and when they got cross they looked particularly funny.

One of Mrs Cats-Home's cats got into such a panic that it ran up a long skirt that was hanging on the washing line, and the line broke. A lot of wet clothes fell on me, and I was still trying to get free of them when Mrs Cats-Home came out of the kitchen. She seemed a bit cross.

"Spud, *really*," she said. "Just *look* at my washing. I'll have to do it all

again, and I'm busy enough
already, what with Angela and the
kittens. You really will have to behave
yourself." And she tied me to the tool-
shed door with a long bit of rope.

It was extremely boring. I dug up
all the plants I could reach, then sat
there, scratching under my chin.
There was nothing else to do.

After a bit, a man opened the gate
and drove a car and trailer in,
backwards. I was still tied up, so I
could only watch. When he'd shut the
gate again, the man shouted, "Anyone
about?"

"Just coming!" Mrs Cats-Home
called from the kitchen. "Get him out,
I'll be with you in a moment."

The man opened the back of the
trailer – and a huge, white animal
with big horns came charging down
the ramp. The man tried to hang onto
its rope, but it knocked him over. I
barked, of course, then wished I hadn't,
because the horrible beast rushed at
me with its head down, and the next
thing I knew, I was being
battered and thumped
as if it wanted to
squash me flat.

The man got to his feet and
grabbed the animal's rope again.
"Hannibal, *leave!*" he shouted. "So
sorry," he added as Mrs Cats-Home
came out. "He's a bit funny about
dogs. I do hope your chap's all right."

Mrs Cats-Home looked at me and asked, "Biscuit?" I stood up and wagged my tail, but she didn't give me a biscuit. "He's fine," she said to the man. "Now, what about Hannibal? Have you brought hay and stuff?" I went and hid behind her skirt.

"Yes, heaps," said the man. "He can sleep in the trailer, it's full of clean straw. Just leave him tethered by your hedge during the day — he'll trim it up for you a treat." And then he unhitched the trailer from his car and drove off.

I was still hiding behind Mrs Cats-Home, and she looked down at me and said, "All right, you can come indoors. But don't you dare chase Angela."

I crept into the kitchen behind her. Angela was purring in a basket with a lot of very tiny kittens. I lay down as far away from her as I could get, and didn't even *look* at her.

Days passed, and I didn't dare go outside on my own. The goat kept breaking its rope, and I never knew when it was waiting for me, or where. One morning, it leapt onto me from the roof of Mrs Cats-Home's car and then chased me all round the garden, and the cats sat and sniggered, safe in their trees. I've never been so embarrassed.

It wasn't much better in the kitchen, because Angela kept rushing out of her basket and spitting at me. She scratched my nose twice, and I got into such a state, my legs were shaking like Geraldine's.

Geraldine and Rosie came every day to take me with them for a walk. We always went to Mrs Piffey's house, because Rosie knew I wanted to see if she was there, but she never was. I began to wonder if she would ever come back.

I gave up chasing the cats because I was too scared of the goat to go outside, and I was very quiet in the kitchen because I was scared of Angela. Mrs Cats-Home said I was very good, and I suppose I was.

One morning three women burst into the kitchen with the goat just behind them. One of them had her arms full of parcels. Mrs Cats-Home jumped up and slammed the door before the goat came in as well – and then I saw who the parcel-woman was.

Mrs Piffey.

I wanted to jump
up and shower her
with kisses, but the
two women with
her were Elsie and
Mavis. What if I had
to go and stay with one of them
again? I tried to hide behind the
vegetable rack.

"Quite good now, isn't he?" said
Mavis. "Amazing."

Mrs Piffey put her parcels on the
table and knelt beside me. "Oh, Spud!"
she said. "What's the matter, darling?
You don't have to be so good any
more, Mama's home!"

I couldn't quite believe it. I sat
beside her while she gave out the
parcels. "Just a few little things," she
said. "Mostly Turkish Delight. But I
brought this for you, Elsie, for looking
after Spud."

Elsie unwrapped a pair of baggy
purple trousers, and a top with fringes
and little gold coins that clinked. She
held them up and stared at them, then
said, "But I didn't look after him."

"Neither did I," said Mavis firmly.
"And I'd much prefer Turkish Delight."
Then she turned to Mrs Cats-Home.
"The purple outfit would be perfect
for you, though, dear. What's your
proper name again?"

"Philomena," said Mrs Cats-Home.
"Philomena Critchley-Hetherington.
And, yes, it's absolutely *wonderful*.
Thank you very much."

She went and put the purple things
on at once, and did a dance in the
kitchen. Mrs Piffey joined in, but
Mavis and Elsie didn't.

★

Things are back to normal now. Mrs Piffey does her hairdressing, and I come and go as I want. I never got any turkey, though. Not even any leftovers – Mrs Piffey and Darling must have eaten every scrap. Mean, really, after I'd been so good about waiting for them to come back. But they took me with them when they went to the seaside the other day, and I found a bin outside a Chinese take-away that smelt almost as good as week-old pigeon. I burped in the car all the way home, and Darling said I was the blooming limit. But Mrs Piffey reached through to the back seat and patted my head. Like I said, she's great.

THE END